THIS WALKER BOOK BELONGS TO:

_____

_____

_____

_____

First published 1987 by
Walker Books Ltd
87 Vauxhall Walk
London SE11 5HJ

This edition published 1989

6 8 10 9 7

© 1987 Colin West

Printed in Hong Kong

British Library Cataloguing in Publication Data
A catalogue record for this book is
available from the British Library.
ISBN 0-7445-1228-X

"Not me,"
said the monkey

Written and illustrated by
Colin West

WALKER BOOKS
AND SUBSIDIARIES
LONDON • BOSTON • SYDNEY

"Who keeps dropping banana skins round here?" growled the lion.

"Not me," said the monkey.

"Who keeps walking all over me?"
hissed the snake.

"Not me," growled the lion.
"And not me," said the monkey.

"Who keeps throwing coconuts about?" snorted the rhino.

"Not me," hissed
   the snake.
"Not me," growled
   the lion.
"And not me,"
   said the monkey.

"WHO KEEPS TICKLING ME?"
roared the elephant.

"Not me," snorted the rhino.
"Not me," hissed the snake.
"Not me," growled the lion.

"And not ME!"
said the monkey.

Slurp! Slurp! Slurp!
went the elephant.

WHOOOOOSH!

"Now who's going to stop
all this monkey business?"
laughed the lion, and the snake
and the rhino, and the elephant

"NOT ME!"
said You-Know-Who.

MORE WALKER PAPERBACKS
For You to Enjoy

Also by Colin West

JUNGLE TALES

Simple, but colourful cumulative stories, each with a
twist in the tail. Ideal for early readers.

0-7445-1065-1   *"Have you seen the crocodile?"*   £4.50
0-7445-1227-1   *"Hello, great big bullfrog!"*   £4.50
0-7445-1229-8   *"Pardon?" said the giraffe*   £4.50
0-7445-1785-0   *Go Tell It to the Toucan*   £4.99

ONE LITTLE ELEPHANT

Elephants sing and surf, skip and skate, jive and juggle
in this most entertaining counting-up rhyme – from one to ten
– which proves that learning can be a jumbo lot of fun!

0-7445-2345-1   £2.99

TEN LITTLE CROCODILES

Crocodiles sail and ski, visit the beach and the zoo,
drop from too much exercise and disappear in a puff of smoke
in this snappy counting-down rhyme – from ten to one
– which shows that learning can be lots of fun!

0-7445-2344-3   £2.99

**Walker Paperbacks are available from most booksellers, or by post
from B.B.C.S., P.O. Box 941, Hull, North Humberside HU1 3YQ**

24 hour telephone credit card line 01482 224626

To order, send: Title, author, ISBN number and price for each book ordered, your full name and address,
cheque or postal order payable to BBCS for the total amount and allow the following for postage and packing:
UK and BFPO: £1.00 for the first book, and 50p for each additional book to a maximum of £3.50.
Overseas and Eire: £2.00 for the first book, £1.00 for the second and 50p for each additional book.

Prices and availability are subject to change without notice.